PALM BEACH COUNTY
LIBRARY SYSTEM
3650 Summit Boulevard
West Palm Beach, FL 33406-4198

Parents and Caregivers,

Stone Arch Readers are designed to provide enjoyable reading experiences, as well as opportunities to develop vocabulary, literacy skills, and comprehension. Here are a few ways to support your beginning reader:

- Talk with your child about the ideas addressed in the story.

- Discuss each illustration, mentioning the characters, where they are, and what they are doing.

- Read with expression, pointing to each word. You may want to read the whole story through and then revisit parts of the story to ensure that the meanings of words or phrases are understood.

- Talk about why the character did what he or she did and what your child would do in that situation.

- Help your child connect with characters and events in the story.

Remember, reading with your child should be fun, not forced. Each moment spent reading with your child is a priceless investment in his or her literacy life.

Gail Saunders-Smith, Ph.D.

STONE ARCH READERS

are published by Stone Arch Books
A Capstone Imprint
1710 Roe Crest Drive
North Mankato, Minnesota 56003
www.capstonepub.com

Library of Congress Cataloging-in-Publication Data
Meister, Cari.
The grumpy lobster / by Cari Meister; illustrated by Steve Harpster.
p. cm. — (Stone Arch readers—ocean tales)
Summary: Arno the lobster is always grumpy and his friends are starting to
avoid him—can he change or will he always be alone?
ISBN 978-1-4342-4025-5 (library binding) — ISBN 978-1-4342-4230-3 (pbk.)
1. Lobsters—Juvenile fiction. 2. Mood (Psychology)—Juvenile fiction. 3.
Friendship—Juvenile fiction. [1. Lobsters—Fiction. 2. Mood (Psychology)—Fiction.
3. Friendship—Fiction.] I. Harpster, Steve, ill. II. Title.
PZ7.M515916Gru 2012
[E]—dc23

2011050082

Art Director: Kay Fraser
Designer: Russell Griesmer
Production Specialist: Kathy McColley

Reading Consultants:

Gail Saunders-Smith, Ph.D.
Melinda Melton Crow, M.Ed.
Laurie K. Holland, Media Specialist

Printed in China
032012   006677RRDF12

The Grumpy LOBSTER

by Cari Meister
illustrated by Steve Harpster

STONE ARCH BOOKS
a capstone imprint

ARNO THE LOBSTER

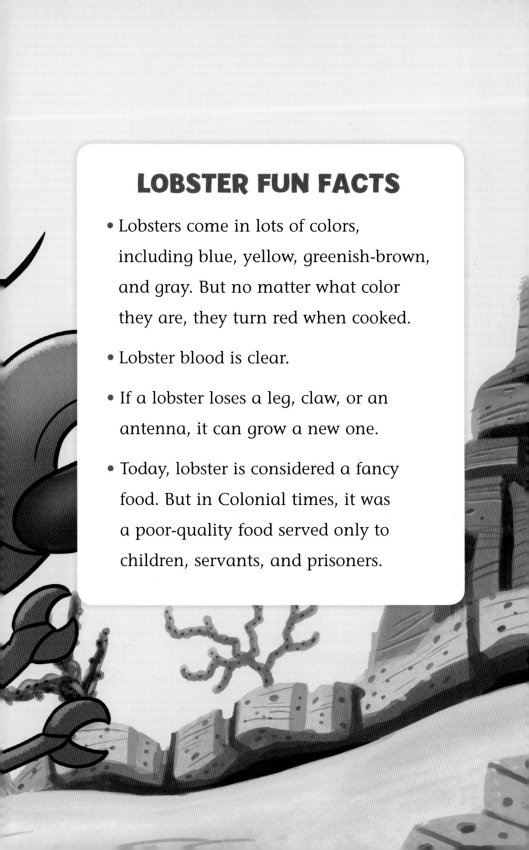

LOBSTER FUN FACTS

- Lobsters come in lots of colors, including blue, yellow, greenish-brown, and gray. But no matter what color they are, they turn red when cooked.

- Lobster blood is clear.

- If a lobster loses a leg, claw, or an antenna, it can grow a new one.

- Today, lobster is considered a fancy food. But in Colonial times, it was a poor-quality food served only to children, servants, and prisoners.

Arno was always grumpy. He
was grumpy when he woke up.

"Squid for breakfast again?"
he said. "Yuck."

Arno was grumpy at school.

"Same dull stuff," he said.
"When will we learn something
interesting?"

Arno was even grumpy at his own birthday party.

"Another year older. Why
should I celebrate?" he asked.

At the spelling bee, Arno won first place. But even that didn't make him happy.

"Good job!" said his teacher. "Here is your prize."

"A shell?" asked Arno. "A shell is my prize?"

He snapped his claw in disgust. "You should give better prizes," he said.

Arno's friends tried to make him feel better.

"Cheer up," said Niki the crab. "It's a great day!"

"What's so great about it?" Arno replied.

"Try to look on the bright side," said Lars the clam.

"There is no bright side," Arno answered. "We live on the dark ocean floor."

After a while, no one wanted
to be around Arno.

"All you do is complain," said
Niki.

"No one wants to be around a grump," said Lars.

Arno swished his fan-like tail
and pushed himself backward.

"Fine! I don't need any
friends!" said Arno. He hid in
a cave.

While he hid in the cave, Arno could hear his friends having a great time.

They raced and played games.
They went midnight hunting.

No one missed Arno or his
grumpiness.

After a few hours, Arno was lonely. He wanted his friends back.

"Nobody likes me," he said.

A starfish heard him.

"Why not?" asked the starfish.

"They say I'm a grump," said Arno.

"Well," said the starfish, "are you?"

But before Arno answered,
the starfish scooted off. Arno
was alone again.

Arno poked out of his hole. He slowly climbed out of the cave.

Arno stuck his legs into the sand and sighed. He knew the answer to the starfish's question.

"Yes!" he said. "I've been a
grump. A big snapping grump!
But not anymore!"

Then he smiled. "If I want my friends back, I need to change my attitude," he said.

Arno called to his friends.
"What are you playing?" he
asked.

"Catch!" said Niki.

"Can I play?" asked Arno.

"Are you sure you want to play?" asked Niki.

"Yes," said Arno. "I'm sorry I've been such a grump!"

Arno played with his friends
for the rest of the day. They all
had a great time.

"Thanks, guys!" said Arno.
"This was the best day ever!"

The next morning, Arno
woke up grumpy. He was about
to complain about breakfast.
But then he remembered the
starfish.

"Squid!" he said. "Sounds tasty!"

The End

STORY WORDS

grumpy	disgust
squid	complain
interesting	midnight
celebrate	attitude

Total Word Count: 430

WHO ELSE IS SWIMMING IN THE OCEAN?

STONE ARCH READERS LEVEL 3
The **Lucky** MANATEE
by Cari Meister
Illustrated by Steve Harpster

STONE ARCH READERS LEVEL 3
The **Clever** DOLPHIN
by Cari Meister
Illustrated by Steve Harpster

STONE ARCH READERS LEVEL 3
The **Stranded** ORCA
by Cari Meister
Illustrated by Steve Harpster